I'm Going To **READ!**™

These levels are meant only as guides;
you and your child can best choose a book that's right.

Level 1: Kindergarten–Grade 1 . . . Ages 4–6

- word bank to highlight new words
- consistent placement of text to promote readability
- easy words and phrases
- simple sentences build to make simple stories
- art and design help new readers decode text

Level 2: Grade 1 . . . Ages 6–7

- word bank to highlight new words
- rhyming texts introduced
- more difficult words, but vocabulary is still limited
- longer sentences and longer stories
- designed for easy readability

Level 3: Grade 2 . . . Ages 7–8

- richer vocabulary of up to 200 different words
- varied sentence structure
- high-interest stories with longer plots
- designed to promote independent reading

Level 4: Grades 3 and up . . . Ages 8 and up

- richer vocabulary of more than 300 different word
- short chapters, multiple stories, or poems
- more complex plots for the newly independent rea
- emphasis on reading for meaning

Note to Parents

What a great sense of achievement it is when you can accomplish a goal! With the **I'm Going To Read!**™ series, goals are established when you pick up a book. This series was developed to grow with the new reader. The vocabulary grows quantifiably from 50 different words at Level One, to 100 different words at Level Two, to 200 different words at Level Three, and to 300 different words at Level Four.

Ways to Use the Word Bank

- Read along with your child and help him or her sound out the words in the word bank.

- Have your child find the word in the word bank as you read it aloud.

- Ask your child to find the word in the word bank that matches a picture on the page.

- Review the words in the word bank and then ask your child to read the story to you.

Related Word Bank Activities

- Create mini-flash cards in your handwriting. This provides yet another opportunity for the reader to be able to identify words, regardless of what the typography looks like.

- Think of a sentence and then place the mini-flash cards on a table out of order. Ask your child to rearrange the mini-flash cards until the sentence makes sense.

- Make up riddles about words in the story and have your child find the appropriate mini-flash card. For example, "It's red and it bounces. What is it?"

- Choose one of the mini-flash cards and ask your child to find the same word in the text of the story.

- Create a second set of mini-flash cards and play a game of Concentration, trying to match the pairs of words.

LEVEL 1

STERLING CHILDREN'S BOOKS
New York

An Imprint of Sterling Publishing
387 Park Avenue South
New York, NY 10016

Lot: 14 15 03/13

Published by Sterling Publishing Co., Inc.
Text © 2005 by Harriet Ziefert Inc.
Illustrations © 2005 by Elliot Kreloff
Distributed in Canada by Sterling Publishing
c/o Canadian Manda Group, 165 Dufferin Street,
Toronto, Ontario, Canada M6K 3H6
Distributed in the United Kingdom by GMC Distribution Services,
Castle Place, 166 High Street, Lewes, East Sussex, England BN7 1XU
Distributed in Australia by Capricorn Link (Australia) Pty. Ltd.
P.O. Box 704, Windsor, NSW 2756, Australia

Sterling ISBN-13: 978-1-4027-2508-1

For information about custom editions, special sales, premium and
corporate purchases, please contact Sterling Special Sales
Department at 800-805-5489 or specialsales@sterlingpub.com.

No More TV, Sleepy Cat

Pictures by Elliot Kreloff

STERLING CHILDREN'S BOOKS
New York

"I'm turning off the TV, Jake."

"I'm not sleepy!" said Jake.
"I want to watch to the end."

"All right. You can watch the end.
Then it's bedtime."

you   bedtime   then

"Jake, it's the end!
Now it's bedtime."

"But I'm not sleepy!"

"I need Fuzzy."

"Fuzzy–all right.
Good night. Sleep tight.
I'm turning off the light."

"But I'm not sleepy!
I need a kiss."

:

"A kiss, all right.
Good night. Sleep tight.
I'm turning off the light."

"But I'm not sleepy!
I need a night light."

"Night light, all right.
Good night. Sleep tight."

"But I'm not sleepy!
I need a drink."

"No drink, Jake!
Good night. Sleep tight.
I'm turning off the light."

**"But I'm not sleepy!
I need a book."**

"No book!
Good night. Sleep tight.
I'm turning off the light."

"But a bedtime book
will make me sleepy."

"Bedtime book.
All right.
Then it's
good night."

you're

"Jake, it's the end.
You're a sleepy . . .
S L E E P Y . . .

sleepy cat!"

STORY

"Sleep tight.
All night."

The
End Z
  z